This Walker book belongs to:

_____

_____

_____

To the Condon family and to Kara,
for living life so generously
M. B.

For Kevin, who has always been a wonderful friend
and a horrible Scrabble player
N. Z. J.

First published 2007 by Walker Books Ltd
87 Vauxhall Walk, London SE11 5HJ

This edition published 2008

2 4 6 8 10 9 7 5 3 1

Text © 2007 Maribeth Boelts
Illustrations © 2007 Noah Z. Jones

The right of Maribeth Boelts and Noah Z. Jones to be identified as author
and illustrator respectively of this work has been asserted by them
in accordance with the Copyright, Designs and Patents Act 1988

This book has been typeset in Univers

Printed in China

British Library Cataloguing in Publication Data:
a catalogue record for this book is available from the British Library

ISBN 978-1-4063-1360-4

www.walkerbooks.co.uk

THOSE SHOES

Maribeth Boelts
illustrated by Noah Z. Jones

WALKER BOOKS
AND SUBSIDIARIES
LONDON · BOSTON · SYDNEY · AUCKLAND

I have dreams about those shoes.
Black high-tops. Two white stripes.

"Grandma, I want them."

"There's no room for 'want' around here – just 'need',"
Grandma says. "And what you *need* are new boots for winter."

Brendon comes to school in those shoes. He says he's the fastest runner now, not me. I used to be the fastest before those shoes came along.

Nat comes to school in those shoes. Tony and I count how many times he goes to the toilet – seven – just so he can walk up and down the corridor *really* slowly.

Next, Alan Jacobs and Terry each get a pair.

Then one day, during sports practice, one of my shoes comes apart.

"Looks like you could do with a new pair, Jeremy," Mr Alfrey, the deputy head, says. He brings out a box of shoes and other stuff he has for kids who need things. He helps me find the only shoes that are my size – Velcro, like the ones my little cousin wears. They have an animal on them, from some cartoon I don't think anyone ever watched.

When I come back to the classroom, Alan Jacobs takes one look at my Mr Alfrey shoes and laughs, and so do Terry, Brendon, and everyone else. The only one not laughing is Tony Parker.

At home, Grandma says, "How kind of Mr Alfrey." I nod and turn my back. I'm not going to cry about some stupid shoes.

But when I'm writing out my spelling words later, every word looks like the word *shoes* and my grip is so tight on my pencil, I think it might break.

On Saturday, Grandma says, "Let's go and look at those shoes you want so much. I've got a bit of money saved up. It might be enough – you never know."

At the shoe shop, Grandma turns those shoes over to
check the price. When she sees it, she sits down heavily.
"Maybe it's wrong?" I say.
Grandma shakes her head.

Then I remember the charity shops.

"Maybe there's a rich boy who's outgrown his or who got two pairs for Christmas and had to give one away?"

We get the bus to the first charity shop. Black cowboy boots, pink slippers, sandals, high heels – all kinds of shoes except the ones I want.

We get the bus to the second charity shop. Not a pair of those shoes in sight.

Round the corner is the third charity shop. I see something in the window...

Black high-tops. Two white stripes.
Perfect shape.
£2.50.

THOSE SHOES.

My heart pounds as I take off my shoes and pull up my saggy socks.

"How exciting!" Grandma says. "What size are they?"

I shove my foot into the first shoe and curl my toes to get my heel in. "I don't know, but I think they fit."

Grandma kneels on the floor and feels for my toes
at the end of the shoe.

"Oh, Jeremy..." she says. "I can't spend good money
on shoes that don't fit."

I pull the other shoe on and try to walk around.

"They're OK," I say, holding my breath and wishing my toes would fall off right there and then.

But my toes don't fall off.

I buy them anyway, with my own money. Then I squeeze them on and limp to the bus stop.

At home, a few days later, Grandma puts a new pair of black boots into my cupboard. She doesn't say a word about my too-big feet hobbling about in my too-small shoes.

"Sometimes shoes stretch," I say. Grandma gives me a hug.

I check every day, but those shoes don't stretch.

I have to wear my Mr Alfreys to school instead.

Then one day, during maths, I notice Tony's shoes.

One of them is taped up. His feet look smaller than mine.

After school, I go to the park to think.
Tony is there – the only one who didn't laugh
at my Mr Alfrey shoes.

We play ball – a loose piece of
tape on Tony's shoe slaps on the
concrete every time he jumps.
    I think, *I'm not going to do it.*

We leap off the swings.
I'm not going to do it.

We race from one end of the playground to the other.
"I'm not going to do it!" I say.
"Do what?" Tony says, breathing hard.

At teatime, Grandma invites Tony in too. After tea, he sees my shoes.

"How come you don't wear them?" Tony asks.

I shrug. My hands are sweaty – I can tell he wishes those shoes were his.

That night, I lie awake for a long time thinking about Tony.
When morning comes, I try on my shoes for the last time.

Before I can change my mind, the shoes are under my jacket.
Snow is beginning to fall as I run across the street to Tony's house.
I put the shoes in front of his door, ring the bell –

and run.

At school, Tony is smiling in his brand-new shoes. I feel happy when I look at his face and cross when I look at my Mr Alfrey shoes.

But later, at breaktime, something happens. There is snow everywhere.

"Leave your shoes in the corridor and change into your boots," the teacher says.

Leave your shoes in the corridor. That's when I remember what I have in my backpack. New boots. New black boots that no one has ever worn before.

Standing in line to go out to break, Tony leans forwards and says, "Thanks."

I smile and give him a nudge...

"Let's race!"

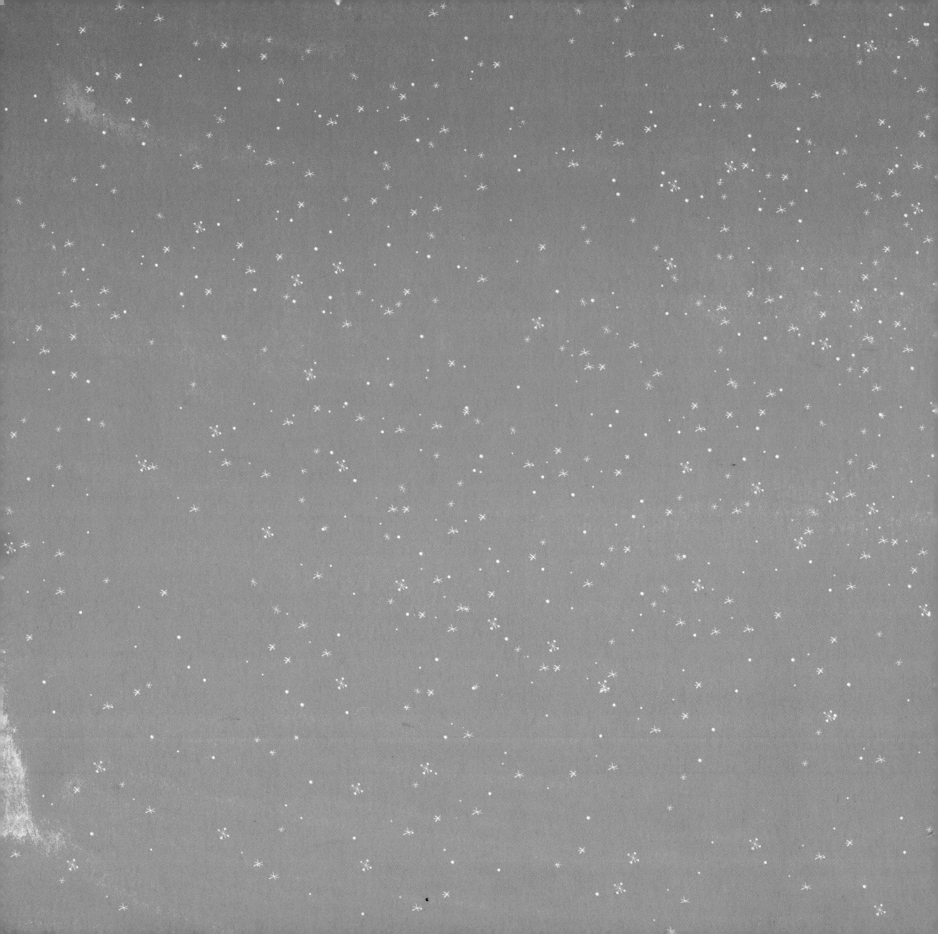

Another title by Noah Z. Jones

NOT NORMAN
A Goldfish Story

Kelly Bennett   illustrated by Noah Z. Jones

ISBN 978-1-84428-288-3

Available from all good bookstores

www.walkerbooks.co.uk